Ben and the Great Big Garden Dig

Justin Scott Parr

GumshoePress

All rights reserved, including the reproduction of this book or portions thereof in any form whatsoever except as provided by the U.S. Copyright Law.

This is a work of fiction. Names, characters, places, and incidents are either the product of the author's imagination or, if real, are used fictitiously.

Text copyright © 2016 Justin Scott Parr
Illustrations and artwork copyright © 2016 GumshoePress

Editor: Carrie White
Illustrated by: Igor Adasikov
Cover Art by: Igor Adasikov, Afreena Rahman
Cover Design by: Svetlana Uscumlic
Interior Design by: Evie Baldwin

ISBN: 978-1-939001-58-0

Please purchase only authorized editions and do not participate in or encourage piracy of copyrighted materials. Your support of the author's rights is appreciated.

Books may be purchased in bulk at special discounts for promotional or educational purposes. Inquiries for sales, distribution, and permissions should be addressed to:

GumshoePress
P.O. Box 1332
New York, NY 10163
support@gumshoepress.com
www.gumshoepress.com

Ben loved gardens.

Big ones and small ones, indoors and outdoors.

He wanted to learn how a garden's fruits and vegetables grow.

But . . .

Some plants grew too high. Others grew too low.

Some plants hid in teeny tiny seeds. Others hid in the dirt.

"How can I help my garden grow if I can't see anything?" Ben wondered.

Then he had an idea.

"I can use my imagination and make believe!"

And then . . .

He crawled into a pea pod.

"Good morning, Ben,"
said the green peas.

"We all look like baby beans in a boat,"
Ben said, sailing inside the pea pod.

"And just like a boat," said the peas,
"we need lots of fresh water."

Then he climbed a tall vine and arrived at a pair of red, ripe tomatoes.

"Are you fruits or vegetables?" he asked.

"Fruits!" shouted one tomato.

"Vegetables!" shouted the other.

Ben saw a group of colorful bell-shaped fruits on a nearby stem.

"We're peppers," they said.

Ben hopped across the green, yellow, orange, and red peppers.

Then he took a bite of a long,
thin pepper. It burned his tongue.

"Call the fire department!" he yelled.

Ben swung across several green stalks. Tucked between their long leaves was a yellow corncob.

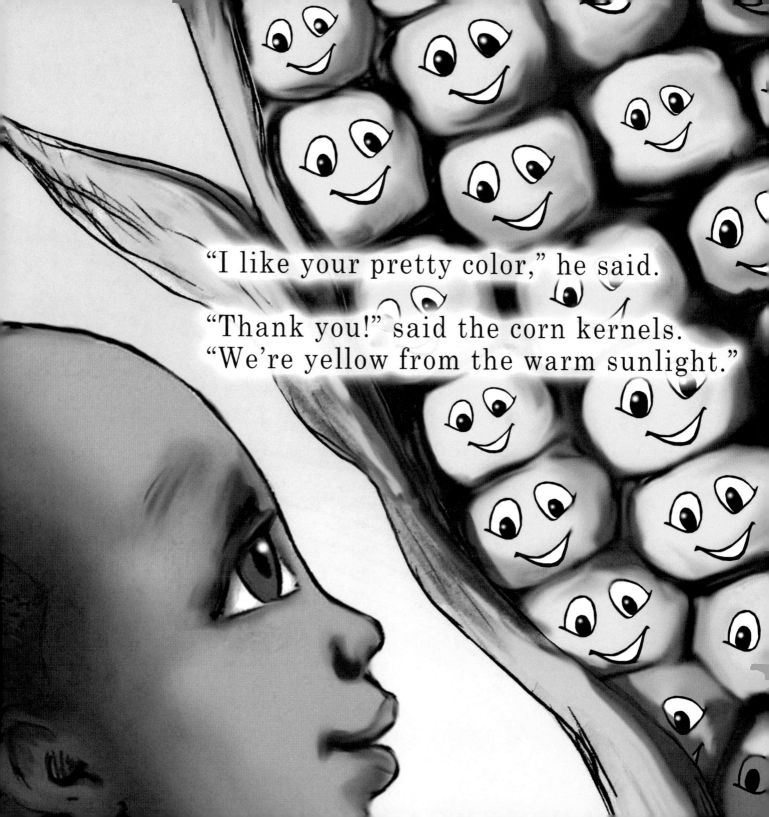

"I like your pretty color," he said.

"Thank you!" said the corn kernels.
"We're yellow from the warm sunlight."

Ben hopped to the ground, and landed
between a row of celery and a pumpkin
patch. He grabbed two celery stalks and
sat down on the biggest orange pumpkin.

"You are my drum and drumsticks," he said, tapping out a beat.

"Join us, Ben!" called some large spinach plants. "We'll keep you cool."

"Your leaves are like huge green fans," said Ben, enjoying the breeze. "And tiny fans, too!"

"We're baby sprouts," the smaller spinach plants replied. "And we need clean air to grow big and strong."

"Tag, you're it!" called the carrots.
"You have to find us, Ben!"

He searched, but couldn't see
who was talking.

Then he crawled
into the ground.

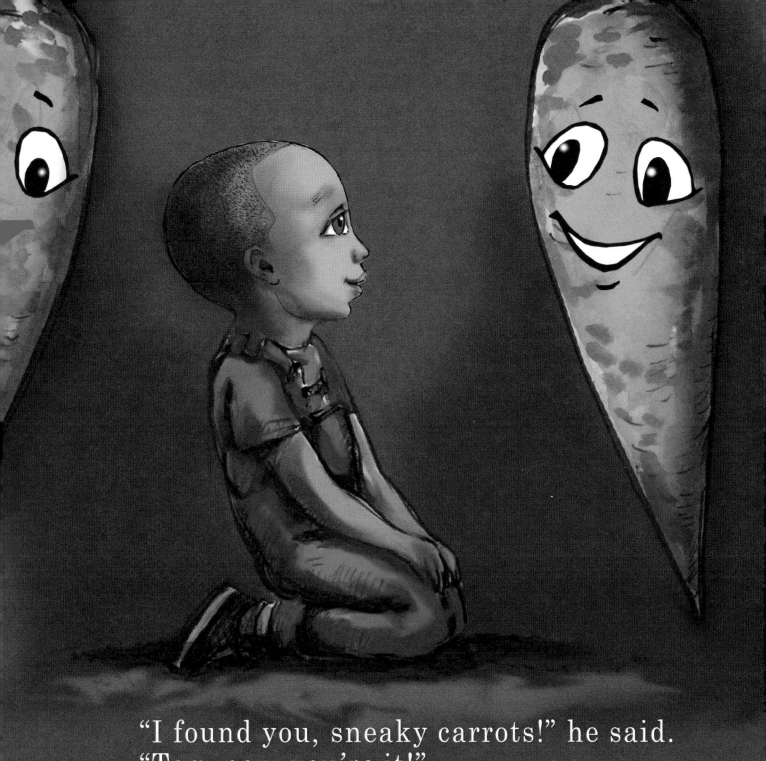

"I found you, sneaky carrots!" he said.
"Tag, now *you're* it!"

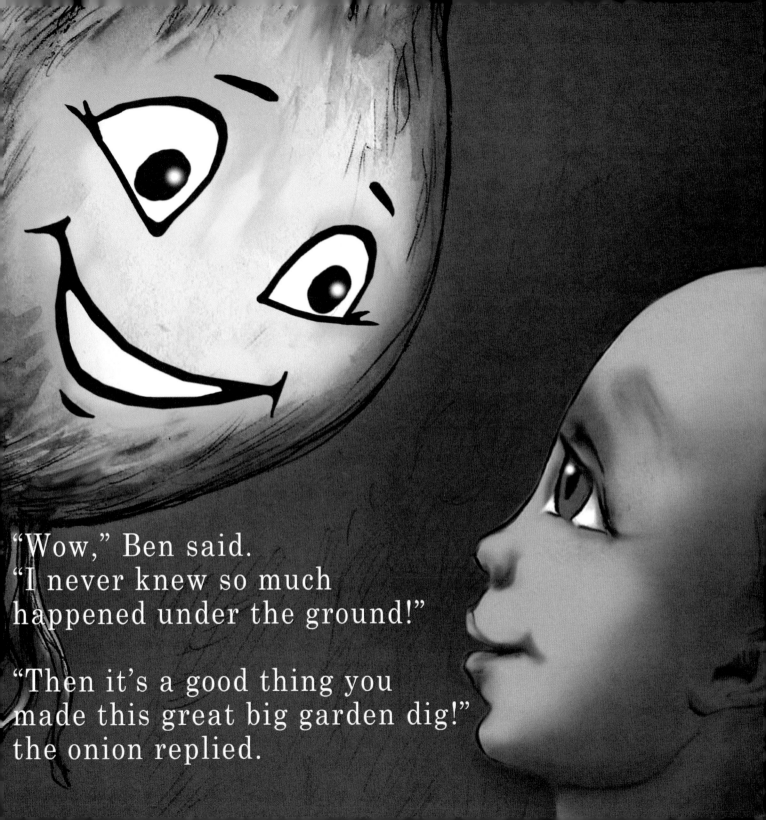

"Wow," Ben said.
"I never knew so much
happened under the ground!"

"Then it's a good thing you
made this great big garden dig!"
the onion replied.

Next, Ben returned to the world above.

Everywhere he looked were colorful vegetables—red, orange, yellow, and green—among the leaves, vines, and roots.

He stretched his arms above his head and pretended he controlled the sun and the clouds.

"I give you all warm sunlight, fresh water, rich soil, and clean air," he said. "Because you are my garden, and *now* I know how you grow!"

To Parents and Educators

THE FOLLOWING RESOURCES are intended to supplement your child's understanding of the concepts in *Ben and the Great Big Garden Dig*. Enjoy these fact pages, craft ideas, outdoor activities, and snack options related to plants.

DID YOU KNOW...

- *Botany* is the study of plant life and a branch of biology.
- *Agriculture* is the practice of farming, which includes caring for the soil and growing plants and other crops.
- A scientist who studies botany is called a *botanist*. Someone who specializes in agriculture is called an *agriculturer* or a *farmer*.
- Plants are alive, just like people and animals.
- Plants come from seeds, and each seed contains a tiny plant waiting for the right conditions to grow, or *germinate*.
- A seed's roots push down into the soil to anchor the new plant and to absorb water and minerals from the soil. Then its stem pushes up toward the sunlight, with new leaves.
- Plants need water, warmth, soil, and light to continue to grow.
- Most plants make their own food directly from sunlight through a process called *photosynthesis*.
- Root vegetables, such as potatoes, carrots, radishes, beets, and turnips, grow under the ground.
- Leafy vegetables such as spinach and lettuce grow above ground.
- The part of broccoli we eat is actually baby flowers that haven't opened yet. Once the flowers open, the broccoli tastes bitter.
- Tomatoes, peppers, green beans, pumpkins, squash, and cucumbers are actually *fruit* because they have seeds inside.

Grow a Garden

GARDENING is not just for grown-ups. It's an activity for kids too. By working in a garden, a child can experience the satisfaction that comes from caring for something over time, while observing the life cycle firsthand.

HERE IS WHAT YOU NEED:
- Garden location
- Garden tools
- Seeds
- Watering can or spray bottle

HERE IS WHAT YOU DO:
- Select a spot for the garden, then help your child to till it.
- Let your child decide which vegetables they would like to grow, then purchase the seeds.
- Read the directions on the seed packets and make a diagram of the garden to outline where to plant different seeds.
- Several days before planting, encourage your child to dig in the dirt with their tools and shovels.
- Let the child make the rows, plant the seeds, and water their garden. (Label each row.)
- Have the child care for their plants by pulling weeds and watering them throughout the year.
- Encourage your child to "harvest" their vegetables and to then prepare them for snack or lunch.

ALTERNATIVE
- If you are unable to create an outdoor garden, then consider making a potted indoor garden in your kitchen or on a windowsill.

Let's Eat!

CUPS OF DIRT
Fill several small cups with instant chocolate pudding. Crush a handful of Oreo cookies (without the cream filling) and pour a layer of crumbled cookies on top of the pudding. Place a gummy worm on top, and enjoy!

RAINBOWS ON A STICK
Collect a variety of colorful vegetables such as carrots, peppers, broccoli, and celery. Cut the vegetables into pieces, and place them onto toothpicks. Be sure to mix up the vegetables so that each toothpick has a variety of colors.

VEGGIE STIR FRY
Cook several cups of rice according to the directions on the package. Heat 1 tbsp of oil in a pan with garlic, onions, and peppers. Cook until soft. Next add carrots, broccoli, peas, and ¼ cup of soy sauce. Add the cooked rice, stir regularly, and cook until vegetables are tender. Enjoy!

Learn a Foreign Language with Ben

Print, ebook, and audiobook editions are available in 7 languages.

Improve FOREIGN-LANGUAGE skills by reading and listening to proper grammar, vocabulary, and pronunciation.

All translations and audiobooks are produced by NATIVE EDITORS and PROFESSIONAL NARRATORS.

EDUCATORS
around the world praise Ben as an effective resource for teaching foreign languages to kids.

LANGUAGES:
- English
- Spanish
- Portuguese
- German
- French
- Italian
- Japanese

Made in the USA
Middletown, DE
19 September 2021

48658884R00020